Diesel's Devious Deed

and Other Thomas the Tank Engine Stories

Based on *The Railway Series* by the Rev. W. Awdry

Photographs by David Mitton and Terry Permane
for Britt Allcroft's production of
Thomas the Tank Engine and Friends

A Random House PICTUREBACK®

Random House 🏠 New York

Library of Congress Cataloging-in-Publication Data
Diesel's devious deed and other Thomas the tank engine stories / photographs by David Mitton and Terry Permane for Britt Allcroft's production of Thomas the tank engine and friends. p. cm.—(A Random House pictureback) "Based on the Railway series by the Rev. W. Awdry." Summary: Diesel causes no end of trouble among the engines when he arrives at Thomas the Tank Engine's train yard. ISBN 0-679-81976-2 (pbk.)—ISBN 0-679-91976-7 (lib. bdg.) [1. Railroads—Trains—Fiction. 2. Behavior—Fiction.] I. Mitton, David, ill. II. Permane, Terry, ill. III. Awdry, W. Railway series. IV. Thomas the tank engine and friends.
PZ7.D5734 1992 [E]—dc20 91-21133

Manufactured in the United States of America 21 22 23 24 25 26 27 28 29 30

Pop Goes the Diesel

Duck is very proud of being Great Western. He talks endlessly about it. But he works hard, too, and makes everything go like clockwork.

It was a splendid day.

The cars and coaches behaved well. The passengers even stopped grumbling!

But the engines didn't like having to bustle about. "There are two ways of doing things," Duck told them. "The Great Western way, or the wrong way. I'm Great Western and—"

"Don't we know it," they groaned.

The engines were glad when a visitor came. He purred smoothly towards them.

Sir Topham Hatt introduced him. "Here is Diesel. I have agreed to give him a trial. He needs to learn. Please teach him, Duck."

"Good morning," purred Diesel in an oily voice. "Pleased to meet you, Duck. Is that James—and Henry—and Gordon too? I am delighted to meet such famous engines."

The silly engines were flattered. "He has very good manners," they murmured. "We are pleased to have him in our yard."

Duck had his doubts. "Come on," he said.
Diesel purred after him.
"Your worthy Top..."
"Sir Topham Hatt to you," ordered Duck.

Diesel looked hurt. "Your worthy Sir Topham Hatt thinks I need to learn. He is mistaken. We diesels don't need to learn. We know everything. We come to a yard and improve it. We are revolutionary."

"Oh!" said Duck. "If you're revo-thingummy, perhaps you would collect my cars while I fetch Gordon's coaches."

Diesel, delighted to show off, purred away.

When Duck returned, Diesel was trying to take some cars from a siding. They were old and empty. They had not been touched for a long time. Diesel found them hard to move.

Pull—push—backwards—forwards! "Oheeeer! Oheeeer!" the cars groaned. "We can't! We won't!"

Duck watched with interest.

Diesel lost patience. "GrrRRRrrrRRR!" he roared, and gave a great heave. The cars jerked forward.

"Oheeeer! Oheeeer!" they screamed. "We can't! We *won't!*" Some of their brakes snapped, and the gear jammed in the sleepers.

"GrrrRRRRrrrrRRRRrrrrRRRR!"

"Ho! Ho! Ho!" chuckled Duck.

Diesel recovered and tried to push the cars back, but they wouldn't move. Duck ran quietly round to collect the other cars. "Thank you for arranging these, Diesel. I must go now."

"Don't you want this lot?"

"No, thank you."

Diesel gulped. "And I've taken all this trouble. Why didn't you tell me?"

"You never asked me. Besides," said Duck, "you were having such fun being rev-whatever-it-was-you-said. Good-bye."

"GrrrRRRrrrRRR!" Diesel had to help the workmen clear the mess. He hated it. All the cars were laughing and singing at him.

"Cars are waiting in the yard; tackling them with ease'll
'Show the world what I can do,' gaily boasts the Diesel.
In and out he creeps about, like a big black weasel.
When he pulls the wrong cars out—pop goes the Diesel!"

"Grrr!" growled Diesel, and scuttled away to sulk in the shed.

Diesel's Devious Deed

Diesel, the new engine, was sulking. The freight cars would not stop singing rudely at him. Duck was horrified. "Shut up!" he ordered, and bumped them hard. "I'm sorry our cars were rude to you, Diesel."

Diesel was still furious. "It's all your fault. You made them laugh at me."

"Nonsense," said Henry. "Duck would never do that. We engines have our differences, but we never talk about them to the cars. That would be dis...dis..."

"Disgraceful!" said Gordon.
"Disgusting!" put in James.
"Despicable!" finished Henry.
Diesel hated Duck. He wanted him to be sent away, so he made a plan. He was going to tell lies about Duck.

Next day he spoke to the cars. "I see you like jokes. You made a good joke about me yesterday. I laughed and laughed. Duck told me one about Gordon. I'll whisper it.... Don't tell Gordon I told you." And he sniggered away.

"Haw! Haw! Haw!" guffawed the cars. "Gordon will be cross with Duck when he knows. Let's tell him and get back at Duck for bumping us."

They laughed rudely at the engines as they went by.

Soon Gordon, Henry, and James found out why.
"Disgraceful!" said Gordon.
"Disgusting!" said James.
"Despicable!" said Henry. "We cannot allow it."
They consulted together. "Yes," they said, "he did it to us. We'll do it to him, and see how he likes it."

Duck was tired out. The cars had been cheeky and troublesome. He wanted to rest in the shed.
The three engines barred his way. "*Hooooooooosh!* Keep out!"

"Stop fooling," said Duck. "I'm tired."

"So are we," hissed the engines. "We are tired of you. We like Diesel. We don't like you. You tell tales about us to the cars."

"I don't."

"You do."

"I don't."

"You do."

Sir Topham Hatt came to stop the noise.

"Duck called me a 'galloping sausage,'" spluttered Gordon.

"…'rusty red scrap iron,'" hissed James.

"…I'm 'old square wheels,'" fumed Henry. "Well, Duck?"

Duck considered. "I only wish, sir," he said gravely, "that I'd thought of those names myself. If the dome fits…"

"He made cars laugh at us," accused the engines.

Sir Topham Hatt recovered. He'd been trying not to laugh himself. "Did you, Duck?"

"Certainly not, sir. No steam engine would be as mean as that."

Diesel lurked up.

"Now, Diesel, you heard what Duck said."

"I can't understand it, sir. To think that Duck, of all engines…I'm dreadfully grieved, sir, but know nothing."

"I see," said Sir Topham Hatt. Diesel squirmed and hoped he didn't.

"I'm sorry, Duck, but you must go to Edward's station for a while. I know he will be glad to see you."

"As you wish, sir."

Duck trundled sadly away while Diesel smirked with triumph.

A Close Shave for Duck

Duck the Great Western Engine puffed sadly to Edward's station. "It's not fair," he complained. "Diesel has been telling lies about me and made Sir Topham Hatt and all the engines think I'm horrid."

Edward smiled. "I know you aren't, and so does Sir Topham Hatt. You wait and see. Why don't you help me with these cars?"

Duck felt happier with
Edward and set to work
at once.

The cars were silly, heavy, and noisy. The two engines had to work
hard, pushing and pulling all afternoon.

At last they reached the top of the hill.

"Good-bye," whistled Duck, and rolled gently over the crossing to the other line.

Duck loved coasting down the hill, running easily with the wind whistling past.

Suddenly— *Tweeeet!*

It was a conductor's warning whistle.

"Hurrah! Hurrah! Hurrah!" laughed the cars. "We've broken away. We've broken away. Chase him, bump him, throw him off the rails," they yelled.

"Hurry, Duck, hurry!" said the driver.

They raced through Edward's station, but the cars were catching up. "As fast as we can—then they'll catch us gradually." The driver was gaining control. "Another clear mile and we'll do it. Oh, glory! Look at that!"

James was just pulling out on their line from the station ahead. Any minute there could be a crash.

"It's up to you now, Duck," cried the driver.

Duck put every ounce of weight and steam against the cars.

"It's too late!" Duck groaned, and shut his eyes. He veered into a siding where a barber had set up shop. He was shaving a customer.

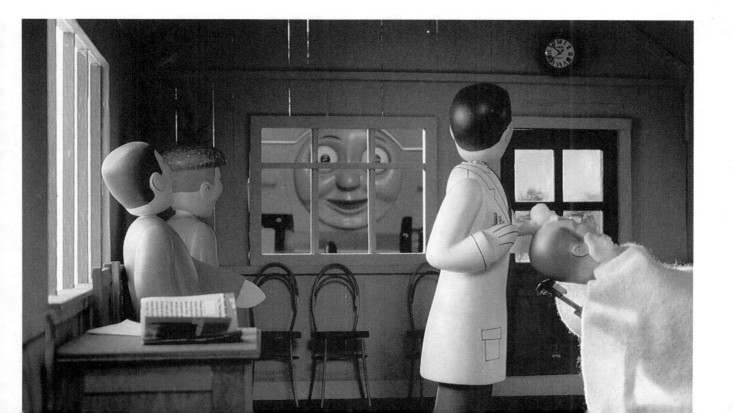

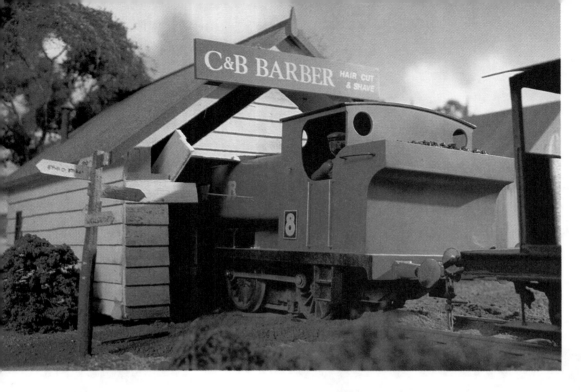

CRASH!

The silly cars had knocked their conductor off his van and left him far behind after he had whistled a warning. But the cars didn't care. They were feeling very pleased with themselves.

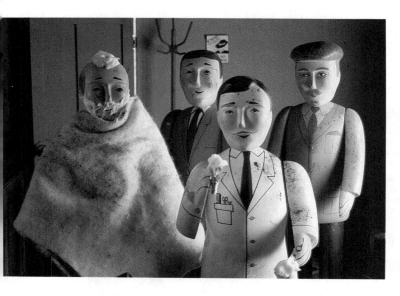

"Beg pardon, sir!" gasped Duck. "Excuse my intrusion."

"No, I won't!" said the barber. "You've frightened my customers. I'll teach you." And he lathered Duck's face all over.

Poor Duck!

Thomas was helping to pull the cars away when Sir Topham Hatt arrived.

"I do not like engines popping through my walls," fumed the barber.

"I appreciate your feelings," said Sir Topham Hatt, "but you must know that this engine and his crew have prevented a serious accident. It was a very close—um—shave!"

"Oh!" said the barber. "Oh, excuse me." He filled a basin of water to wash Duck's face. "I'm sorry. I didn't know you were being a brave engine."

"That's all right, sir. I didn't know that either."

"You were very brave indeed," said Sir Topham Hatt. "I'm proud of you."

Sir Topham Hatt watched the rescue operation. Then he had more news for Duck. "And when you are properly washed and mended, you are coming home."

"Home, sir? Do you mean the yard?"

"Of course."

"But, sir, they don't like me. They like Diesel."

"Not now. I never believed Diesel, so I sent him packing. The engines are sorry and want you back."

A few days later when he came home, there was a really rousing welcome for Duck the Great Western Engine.

Woolly Bear

In the summer the work crews cut the long grass along the tracks—raking it into heaps to dry in the sun.

At this time of year, Percy stops where they have been cutting. The men load up his empty wagons, and he pulls them to the station.

Toby then takes them to the hills for the farmers to feed their stock.

"*Wheeeeeeesh*!" Percy gave a ghostly whistle. "Don't be frightened, Thomas." He laughed. "It's only me!"

"Your ugly fizz is enough to frighten anyone," said Thomas. "You're like—"

"Ugly indeed! I'm—"

"—a green caterpillar with red stripes," continued Thomas firmly. "You crawl like one too."

"I don't!"

"Who's been late every afternoon this week?"

"It's the hay."

"I can't help that," said Thomas. "Time's time, and Sir Topham Hatt relies on me to keep it. I can't if you crawl in the hay till all hours."

" 'Green caterpillar' indeed!" fumed Percy as he set off to collect some hay to take to the harbor. "Everyone says I'm handsome—or at least nearly everyone. Anyway, my curves are better than Thomas's corners. Thomas says I'm always late," he grumbled. "I'm never late—or at least only a few minutes. What's that to Thomas? He can always catch up time farther on."

All the same, he and his driver decided to start home early. Then came trouble.

CRASH!
A crate of treacle was upset all over Percy.
Percy was cross. He was still sticky when he puffed away.

The wind was blowing fiercely.

"Look at that!" exclaimed the driver.

The wind caught the piled hay, tossing it up and over the track.

The line climbed here. "Take a run at it, Percy," his driver advised.

Percy gathered speed. But the hay made the rails slippery, and his wheels wouldn't grip. Time after time he stalled with spinning wheels and had to wait until the line ahead was cleared before he could start again.

Everyone was waiting.
Thomas seethed impatiently.
"Ten minutes late! I warned
him. Passengers'll complain,
and Sir Topham Hatt..."

Then they all saw Percy. They laughed and shouted.
"Sorry I'm late!" Percy panted.

"Look what's crawled out of the hay!" teased Thomas.

"What's wrong?" asked Percy.

"Talk about hairy caterpillars!" puffed Thomas. "It's worth being late to have seen you."

When Percy got home, his driver showed him what he looked like in a mirror.

"Bust my buffers! No wonder they all laughed. I'm just like a woolly bear! Please clean me before Toby comes." But it was no good. Thomas told Toby all about it.

Instead of talking about sensible things like playing ghosts, Thomas and Toby made jokes about "woolly bear" caterpillars and other creatures which crawl about in hay.

They laughed a lot, but Percy thought they were really being very silly indeed.